RULE!

The Night
of the Chipmunk

Read all the **Pets RULE!** books

1
Pets RULE!
My Kingdom of Darkness

2
Pets RULE!
The Poodle of Doom

3
Pets RULE!
Kittens Are Monsters

4
Pets RULE!
The Rise of The Goldfish

5
Pets RULE!
Invasion of the Pugs

6
Pets RULE!
The Night of the Chipmunk

7
Pets RULE!
Revenge of the Raccoons

Pets RULE!

The Night of the Chipmunk

Written by
Susan Tan

Illustrated by
Wendy Tan Shiau Wei

BRANCHES

SCHOLASTIC INC.

To Buddy Dog and all other superheroes – ST

To Lucky, my precious baby – WTSW

Text copyright © 2024 by Susan Tan
Illustrations copyright © 2024 by Wendy Tan Shiau Wei

Library of Congress Cataloging-in-Publication Data

Names: Tan, Susan, author. | Wei, Wendy Tan Shiau, illustrator. |
Tan, Susan. Pets rule ; 6.
Title: The night of the chipmunk / Susan Tan ; illustrated by Wendy Tan Shiau Wei.
Description: First edition. | New York : Branches/Scholastic, 2024. |
Series: Pets rule! ; 6 | Audience: Ages 6–8. | Audience: Grades 2–3. |
Summary: Ember the Chihuahua, his humans, and his friends are spending a
few days on Acorn Island—which is rumored to be ruled by a giant, evil
chipmunk, determined to drive away all humans and pets.
Identifiers: LCCN 2023041892 (print) |
ISBN 9781546119746 (paperback) | ISBN 9781546119753 (library binding) |
Subjects: LCSH: Chihuahua (Dog breed)—Juvenile fiction. | Dogs—Juvenile
fiction. | Chipmunks—Juvenile fiction. | Animals—Juvenile fiction. |
Humorous stories. | CYAC: Chihuahuas (Dog breeds)—Fiction. |
Dogs—Fiction. | Chipmunks—Fiction. | Animals—Fiction. | Humorous
stories. | LCGFT: Humorous fiction. | Animal fiction.
Classification: LCC PZ7.1.T37 Ni 2024 (print) |
DDC 813.6 [Fic] —dc23/eng/20230912
LC record available at https://lccn.loc.gov/2023041892

ISBN 978-1-5461-1975-3 (hardcover) / ISBN 978-1-5461-1974-6 (paperback)

10 9 8 7 6 5 4 3 2 1   24 25 26 27 28

Printed in China 62
First edition, October 2024
Edited by Cindy Kim
Cover design by Brian LaRossa
Book design by Jaime Lucero

Table of Contents

The Chin Family VACATION

Mr. Chin

Mrs. Chin

Kevin

CHAPTER 1

The Road to . . . Chaos?

It was a beautiful day in the park. The Chin family, and my favorite human, Lucy, were having a big picnic with Arjun's and Lia's families. My five new pug friends were there too. I had thought Ravioli and his brothers and sisters were aliens trying to take over Earth. But it turns out, they're just dogs like me.

1

"We made a last-minute booking for Acorn Island," Mr. Chin said. "Ember, Izzy, and Sweet Pea can come along. We leave tomorrow!"

I had just found out that my human family was going on vacation with Lia's and Arjun's families.

This was very good news, for I am Ember the Mighty. I'm going to rule the world someday. And now I would get to see more of my future kingdom.

But the pugs looked at me with scared eyes.

"You can't go! Acorn Island is haunted," Ravioli said. "By an evil chipmunk!"

"Please, I can handle a chipmunk," I said.

"No, you don't understand," Ravioli said. "They call her the Monster of Acorn Island! She haunts the night and is believed to have magical powers. Legends say that she won't rest until she's scared everyone off the island."

"Wait, the chipmunk has magic pow—?" I began to ask. But I didn't have time to finish. All the humans started packing up the picnic.

"We should all probably head home now," Mrs. Chin said. "We need to get ready for tomorrow."

So Lucy led me away, along with Lia and Arjun. And I said goodbye to the pugs.

"I'm so excited! I can't believe we're going on a vacation together!" Lucy said to her friends. I was happy I'd have pets to go with, too. Sweet Pea, the frog, lived with Lia and her family, and Izzy was Arjun's sheepdog.

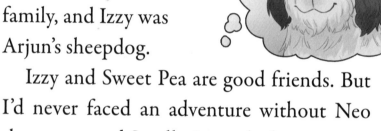

Izzy and Sweet Pea are good friends. But I'd never faced an adventure without Neo the canary and Smelly Steve the hamster.

"I love the pet sitter! And I know you're going to have a great time," Steve said.

"Yeah, Acorn Island sounds like a lot of fun!" Neo added.

I knew they were right. I was going to miss them a lot. But we'd all have stories to tell one another when we got back.

So I really wanted to be more excited. But going to an island where an evil chipmunk haunts the night did NOT sound fun.

But at least Lucy was excited for tomorrow.

She could swim all day and build the biggest sandcastle ever!

Seeing her happy made me feel a bit calmer. Maybe if I stayed close to her, everything would be fine.

"You'll be okay, right, Ember?" Steve asked in a worried tone.

"I'm sure I'll be fine," I said as we pulled up to the Chin house.

"Yeah, don't worry," Neo said. "There's no such thing as monsters or giant evil chipmunks."

"Uh, exactly," I said, my voice a little shaky. "Everything will be okay!"

Being back home made me feel much better until . . . a loud, awful sound came out of nowhere!

DING DONG—SCREEEEECH!!!!!!

CHAPTER 2

Little Shop of Cheese

"AAAAAAAH!" I screamed. WHAT IS THAT?

I looked up to see an ENORMOUS, tall shadow looming over me, Neo, and Steve.

"Oh, hi, Linda!" Mr. Chin said as he opened the door.

"Hello, Mr. Chin! I think your doorbell might be broken—it sounds way out of tune," Linda said.

Phew! It was just the doorbell, and Linda, the family pet sitter. Thank goodness!

But if Linda was here, that meant Neo and Steve were leaving right now. I rushed over to give my friends a big hug.

"Goodbye, faithful hamster. Goodbye, brave bird. I will miss you," I said.

"I'll miss you, too, Ember!" Steve wailed.

"We'll see you soon, Ember!" Neo said, giving me a feathery hug.

Mr. Chin handed Linda a box with food for both Neo and Steve. Then I watched as Neo and Steve got into their cages. With one last wave, they headed out the door.

Now, it was time for the humans to pack.

"I found the volleyball net!" Mr. Chin said happily, holding up a duffel bag.

"Mr. Ramanathan, Arjun's dad, is going to teach me how to bake hamburger rolls!" Kevin said, packing his pans.

"I found the s'more sticks," Mrs. Chin said. She held up a bundle of long carved sticks, which had CHIN FAMILY written on the side.

"And I'm going to find so many rocks!" Lucy said, holding up her magnifying glass. Lucy is going to be a geologist someday (along with ruling the world with me, of course).

Once the humans were packed, we had dinner, and then it was time for bed. I had decided that we were going to have a great trip. Neo was right—there was no such thing as giant evil chipmunks. There was no need to be nervous.

I curled up on Lucy's pillow and closed my eyes. Before I knew it, morning came and it was time to go.

I followed Lucy out to the driveway. Lia's and Arjun's families were already waiting for us outside.

Dr. Ramanathan helped load our suitcases into the car. Lia's dad, Mr. Baptiste, handed out snacks, while Lia's mom and Mrs. Chin figured out the best route.

"Hi, Ember!" Sweet Pea called from her tank.

"Ready for a road trip?" Izzy asked.

We waited while the humans packed up the cars. My pet friends and I rode in Mr. Baptiste's car with Lucy and her friends. Everyone else piled into the second car that Mr. Chin was driving.

There were so many new smells and things to see out the window. After riding for a while, we stopped at a gas station that had cheese snacks EVERYWHERE.

"When I rule the world, we will eat cheese every day!" I told Lucy.

Lucy snuck me another piece of cheese, so I could tell she was excited, too.

With my belly full, I was feeling very happy as we drove over the bridge that led to Acorn Island.

"Wow!" Mrs. Baptiste said. "You can see the whole island from here."

The humans rolled down their windows. All the pets and I looked up in awe. A beautiful, green island was waiting for us.

But before I could get a better look, I heard a small voice from just outside the window.

"Turn back now, before it's too late!" the voice whispered.

CHAPTER 3

A Bridge WAY Too Far

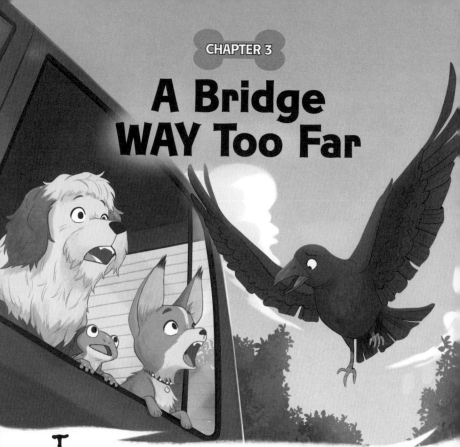

I zzy, Sweet Pea, and I stood up and looked out the open car window.

There was a big black raven, flying next to the car!

"Turn back!" it cawed again. "Beware of Acorn Island."

"What, why?!" Sweet Pea asked.

But just then, the minivan sped up, and the mysterious bird moved away.

"Wait, come back!" I barked.

But the raven flew up into the sky, calling out to us again.

"The Monster of Acorn Island lurks in the night! Be careful in the woods," the raven cawed.

Then, the bird disappeared behind the clouds.

My fur stood straight up. The island, which had seemed so beautiful and green a moment ago, now seemed shadowy and scary.

"That was so strange!" Sweet Pea said.

Sweet Pea and Izzy hadn't been warned like I had. So I told them what the pugs had told me about the Monster of Acorn Island.

"Hmmm. I've read lots of scary stories, but none of them have evil chipmunks. Are you sure this is real?" Sweet Pea asked.

"Why would the raven warn us if it wasn't real?!" Izzy asked.

"Exactly!" I said, nodding my head.

"Hmmm," Sweet Pea said. She didn't look convinced. But there was no turning back now!

"As long as we stay out of the woods, we'll be fine, right?" Izzy asked. "That's what the raven just said—stay out of the woods at night."

My ears perked up.

"Excellent plan, Izzy!" I said. "All we have to do is avoid the woods."

"Welcome to the island!" Mr. Baptiste said as the car pulled off the main road, down a dirt path labeled ACORN CABINS.

"We're almost there! Three days in the woods, away from all cell phone service! Get excited!" Mrs. Baptiste said.

That's when my stomach fell. The path led directly into a forest of tall, looming trees.

Three days trapped in the woods with an evil chipmunk on the loose?

"Oh no, we're DOOMED!" Izzy gasped.

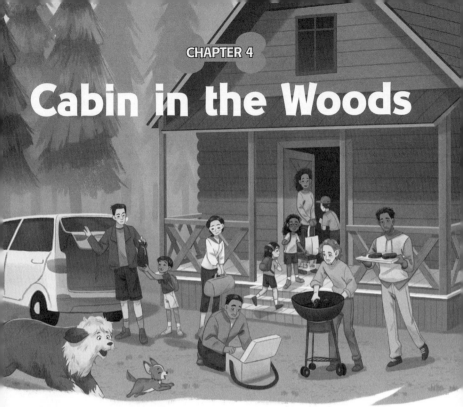

CHAPTER 4

Cabin in the Woods

The car pulled up to a big wooden cabin. There was a large yard and a porch.

Arjun's dad was already in the yard, setting up for tonight's barbecue on the grill. The other humans got out of the car and started to unpack.

Izzy and I began to sniff around, while Lia set Sweet Pea's tank on the porch.

There were wildflowers at the edge of the clearing, and grass and plants everywhere.

It was beautiful.

I took another deep sniff. Maybe this trip wasn't going to be so bad after all.

Then, I heard a strange rustling.

"What was that?" Izzy asked.

"I don't know," I said.

The sound was coming from the side of the cabin.

There was a rustle again and then a scraping noise. I looked behind me. Lucy and Kevin and the rest of the humans were right there, just a few steps away. Now felt like the time to be brave.

"Let's go see what it is," I said to Izzy. "Maybe it's just the wind."

We crept to the side of the cabin.

"On the count of three," I whispered to Izzy. The sounds were so close to us. I knew that if we turned the corner, we'd see what was making the noise.

"One, two . . . three!" I said.

We jumped around the cabin.

There was no one there.

But there *was* something left behind, in the grass.

They were long carved sticks. They were broken and scattered all over.

And on the side of the sticks was a name I recognized: CHIN FAMILY.

That's when I heard a gasp from behind me.

"Oh no, all the s'mores sticks are broken!" Kevin said.

"Bad dogs!" Mr. Chin said.

"But how did Ember and Izzy even get to the s'mores sticks?" Lucy asked. "The sticks were in a bag, and the dogs know not to go digging into our things."

"Yeah, that's weird," Arjun said. "Izzy never breaks things at home."

"Yes, exactly!" Izzy barked happily.

But somehow, both of us pets were still blamed for the mess.

Izzy and I were put on our leashes and had to stay by the porch.

When the humans left, we told Sweet Pea what had happened.

"But I've been on the porch this whole time! Neither of you were up here. And why would you want to break the sticks?" Sweet Pea asked.

It all felt very unfair. Was someone trying
to get us in trouble?

I didn't know. But one thing was for sure:
there was something TERRIFYING in these
woods.

And night was about to fall.

CHAPTER 5

What Pets Do in the Shadows

For the rest of the night I stayed right next to Lucy, and Izzy stuck close to Arjun. Sweet Pea wasn't convinced that we were dealing with a real haunting, but she would croak whenever Lia went too far away.

The humans grilled for dinner and decided to save s'mores for another day.

I was so happy when it was time for bed. I had spent the whole day imagining scary things everywhere. Luckily, I knew I'd be safe with Lucy.

I curled up on Lucy's pillow. I closed my eyes and tried to fall asleep.

But then—

Scratch . . . scratch . . .

I bolted up. There was a noise coming from outside.

"Pretend it's not there," I told myself.

Scratch . . . scratch . . . The noise continued.

I tried to put my ears under the pillow. But I could still hear the noise.

It was no use. I knew I wouldn't be able to sleep if I didn't see what was going on. And besides, I'm a future dark overlord. How can I rule the world if I can't face a chipmunk?

I crept out of bed, and left the room that Lucy and Lia were sharing.

"Psst, Ember!" Izzy whispered from behind me. She tiptoed out of the room that Kevin and Arjun were sharing. "Did you hear that noise?"

"Yeah, I heard it!" Sweet Pea said, hopping out of her tank to join us.

Together, we crept outside.

It was so dark it was hard to see anything. The only light was from the moon.

"Oh no, the grill!" Sweet Pea said. "It's knocked over!"

"And that's all the firewood our humans had stacked!" Izzy said. The firewood was EVERYWHERE. It was like a giant creature had picked up the logs and tossed them like Frisbees.

"But what could do this?" I asked.

Then, as I spoke, a dark shadow fell over us.

I couldn't see it clearly at first. But then the moonlight got brighter. Right in front of us was a GIANT  CHIPMUNK, even taller than Izzy. And a long cloak fluttered behind it.

"Foolish pets! You are no match for me!" the giant chipmunk proclaimed. "BWAHAHAHAHA!"

And then it disappeared into the darkness.

"The Monster of Acorn Island! It's real!" I gasped.

CHAPTER 6

The Scary Plan

We had just seen the chipmunk that haunts Acorn Island, and it was ENORMOUS. Izzy, Sweet Pea, and I stood frozen in place.

I was so scared that I didn't hear the porch door open behind me.

"Ember, no!" Lucy gasped, looking at the big mess. Arjun and Lia rushed over, too.

Once again, somehow, it looked like *we'd* caused trouble.

"BAD PETS," Mr. Chin said, joining Lucy on the porch.

I wasn't allowed back in Lucy's room. Instead, the humans put me and Izzy in the kitchen as punishment.

I lay in my dog bed, trying to sleep. Every sound outside made me jump.

The chipmunk is just so scary! I thought to myself. *I hate being scared! And if I'm going to rule the world someday, I need to be the scary one—*

That was it!

I smiled as I drifted off to sleep. I had a plan.

The next morning the humans had breakfast and then went to swim. Mr. Chin tied our leashes to a tree by the lake, and Lia put Sweet Pea's tank nearby.

As they swam, I told Izzy and Sweet Pea my plan.

"This chipmunk is ruining our vacation, and she won't stop until we're blamed for everything that goes wrong!" I said. "We have to defeat her, and I know how."

"How?" Izzy asked.

"We need to become just as scary!" I declared. "Then the chipmunk will know not to mess with us."

"Good idea," Izzy said.

"But I don't think we should be scary on purpose," Sweet Pea said. "That's mean."

"We're going up against a giant evil chipmunk! What else can we do?" I asked.

"We can ask questions, and try to be better than the chipmunk," Sweet Pea said. "That's what all the characters in my favorite superhero books do, and it always works."

"This isn't a book!" I said, interrupting her. "I know you love reading, but it's time to take action. We have to do something to protect our humans!"

I could tell I'd hurt Sweet Pea's feelings. But I didn't know how to fix it.

"I think we need to find out more," Izzy said. She looked sad, like she was trying to stop us from fighting.

"Maybe there are other animals in the woods who can tell us what's going on," Izzy added.

"Good idea," I said quietly.

"Okay," Sweet Pea said, not looking at me.

Izzy and I slipped off our leashes as Sweet Pea hopped out of her tank, and the three of us snuck away.

As we did, I saw Lucy playing with Lia and Arjun in the lake. She was so happy. And it was my job to protect her and keep her from scary things. I *had* to follow my plan and become as scary as the chipmunk.

So I took a deep breath and walked into the woods.

After a few minutes, we stopped by a small pond and looked around. There was no one there. But the fur on my back stood up. I knew we weren't alone.

I turned to look at the still pond . . .

And saw a pair of eyes, staring back at me!

CHAPTER 7

Junk Scare

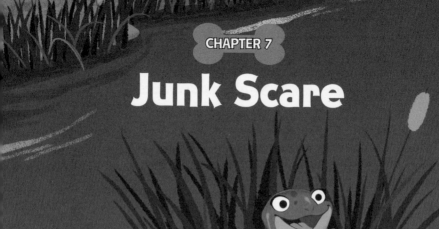

Two big eyes stared up at us from the pond. It was a frog!

"Hey there, fellow frog!" Sweet Pea called out. "Who are you?"

"I'm Greta," the frog said. "Welcome to Acorn Island!"

"Hi, Greta! I'm Sweet Pea, and these are my friends, Izzy and Ember," Sweet Pea said.

"We're here on serious business. We need to find the Monster of Acorn Island," I added.

Greta gasped.

"No one in these woods speaks of her," she began. "She used to be my friend. But one day, she decided to rule our home and scare all the animals and new humans! Now my friends avoid this pond."

"How do you think we can stop her? We'd like to help," I replied.

"I'm not sure. But you should ask the wise old owl. She's awake all night and sees everything. I bet she will know," Greta said.

Greta told Sweet Pea how to find the owl, and we waved goodbye. We were heading back toward the lake when suddenly—

"OH NO!" Lucy yelled from somewhere close by.

"This is terrible!" Arjun said.

"Come on! Our humans are in trouble!" I shouted.

"ARJUN!" Izzy barked.

"LIA!" Sweet Pea cried.

We raced toward the voices.

I ran in front of Lucy, my fur on end. Izzy leapt in front of Arjun in her best dance-fight pose. Sweet Pea puffed her chest like a balloon as she hopped in front of Lia.

We were ready to take on whatever evil threatened our humans.

But there was no one there!

"This is terrible!" Lucy said angrily.

"Who would do this?" Lia demanded.

We found Lucy and her friends standing in a clearing that was littered with trash.

I let out a big sigh. Our humans weren't in trouble. They'd been yelling because they were upset.

I wanted to help Lucy, so I picked up a snack wrapper and brought it over.

Lucy thanked me. Then she and her friends started picking up trash, too. But there was so much of it! Old candy wrappers, plastic bags, and cartons that had once held graham crackers covered the ground.

Soon, the adults and Kevin came to join them.

"Dad, look!" Lucy said.

"Oh no! This is not good," Mr. Chin said.

"We have to do something!" Kevin said.

"Wow, we've been left with quite a mess," Mr. Chin said. "Sadly, not everyone cleans up their own trash."

Everyone nodded in agreement.

"That's not right!" Arjun cried. "They're hurting the forest. Who would do that?"

Right then, I looked down at the ground and noticed a long trail of tiny footprints.

I gasped. That's when it all clicked. I knew EXACTLY who would hurt the forest.

"It's the Monster of Acorn Island," I whispered to my friends. "It has to be. Look at these paw prints!"

"I don't know. Are you sure?" Sweet Pea asked.

"Yes, it's the evil chipmunk. We have to stop her, or the whole forest will suffer!" I declared.

"What do we do?" Izzy asked.

"We need to go see the owl as soon as night falls and the humans go to bed," I replied. "It's time to defeat evil."

CHAPTER 8

Silence of the Owls

We went back to our cabin. After dinner, Lucy took me for a walk.

Normally, Lucy and I love going on walks. But with an evil chipmunk on the loose, I knew it was my duty to keep her safe. So I pulled on my leash to go back to the cabin.

When we got back, Lucy put me and Izzy in the kitchen again before going to bed. I was exhausted, but I didn't let myself fall asleep.

Once all the lights were off, Izzy and I tiptoed to the porch door. Sweet Pea hopped down to meet us. She seemed extra quiet.

I wondered if she didn't like my plan for us to become just as scary as the chipmunk.

But still, Sweet Pea led the way, following Greta's directions through the woods. We passed through tangled bushes and tall, looming trees.

Suddenly, as I looked up at the tall shadows in the trees, I felt scared. So I reminded myself that the woods wouldn't be scary anymore once we defeated the chipmunk. Then, these woods could become part of MY kingdom!

We reached a giant tree with long, winding branches.

"This is it," Sweet Pea said. "This is where the owl should be."

We looked up. There was no one there.

"Are you sure?" I asked. "I don't see—"

SWOOSH.

Something ENORMOUS swooped over our heads.

Then the owl landed on a branch.

"WHO DISTURBS ME?!" the owl demanded.

I bared my teeth and tried to look strong and fierce. That's when Sweet Pea calmly stepped forward.

"Hello, wise owl," she said politely. "We're sorry to bother you. We need some help. Greta the frog sent us!"

I waited for the owl to say something mean.

But the owl just blinked and gave a soft hoot.

"I'm sorry. You just scared me," the owl said in a much nicer voice. "I'm Ollie. How can I help you?"

Sweet Pea took a deep breath and then started to explain.

Then Ollie told us, "The chipmunk lives in an old oak tree. There's a wide network of birds here on Acorn Island. Many of us have seen her come in and out."

I wanted to ask more about this bird network, since it sounded very useful for when I rule the world. But Ollie kept going.

"In fact, the chipmunk lives right by the cabin where you are staying. I don't know how she grew so big and strong. But I do know that she has one weakness—daylight! If you face her during the day, you may stand a chance of defeating her."

"Thank you, Ollie," I said. "When I rule the world, you will be rewarded."

"How lovely!" Ollie hooted. "Let me know how it goes with the chipmunk!"

We promised we would, and then headed back to our cabin.

"It's official," I said. "We will still use my same plan, but now we'll stage a surprise attack tomorrow!"

CHAPTER 9

The Invitation

Izzy, Sweet Pea, and I tiptoed back to the cabin. Luckily, no one heard us or woke up.

The next morning, Lucy took me for my walk, and then everyone had breakfast.

"So, I've been thinking about the litter. We should clean it up," Lucy said.

"Yes! But cleaning it up won't solve the problem. We need to make signs, saying not to litter," Lia said.

"I agree, but creating signs alone isn't good enough," Arjun said. "There have to be official rules about littering. We should write a letter to the mayor in charge of this island."

"Good idea!" Kevin replied.

"Yes, great idea, I think making signs will help," Mr. Chin said.

"But remember, we can't fix this littering problem in a weekend," Lia's dad added. "You kids should still have fun."

"Yeah, maybe we don't need to clean up the litter right away," Kevin agreed. "It's not *our* mess."

"But, Kevin! You should help us," Lucy said, now upset at her brother.

I could tell Kevin wasn't happy.

"We're on vacation. Not at some cleanup boot camp!" Kevin replied, frustrated.

Then, before I knew it, everyone was arguing about what to do.

It was official—this vacation was a disaster! And it was all the evil chipmunk's fault!

If there was anyone who was going to stop this chipmunk, it was going to be me and my friends.

After breakfast, all the humans left for the lake. Lia, Arjun, and Lucy were quiet, and no one was laughing. They left all of us pets at the cabin this time, which was perfect.

It was time for Izzy, Sweet Pea, and I to set my plan into motion. We were going to become bigger and scarier than the chipmunk! I could tell Sweet Pea didn't love it. But we didn't have any better ideas, so she agreed to try.

Izzy found Mrs. Chin's volleyball net and a flashlight. I tugged on Mr. Chin's bathroom towel that was hanging on the wall. Sweet Pea took a piece of paper from Lia's sketching journal. Then we made our way to the giant oak tree.

"Positions!" I whispered.

Izzy wrapped the volleyball net around the tree. Then I climbed onto Izzy's head. I wrapped the towel around my shoulders. Within seconds, we looked like one GIANT dog, with our very own evil cape!

Sweet Pea took the flashlight and found a small hole at the bottom of the oak tree. We knew that must be the doorway inside.

I nodded to Sweet Pea to give her the signal. We were ready to face the chipmunk!

She turned the light on and directed it . . . right into the tree! We knew this would flood the monster's nest with light, forcing it to come outside.

I rolled the piece of sketch paper into a megaphone.

"MONSTER OF ACORN ISLAND!" I boomed, sounding as scary as I could. "I am Ember, future ruler of this world! I challenge you to a scare-off!"

For a moment, I thought it wouldn't work.

Suddenly, there was a skittering sound. Something ran from the tree . . . right into the volleyball net!

But the figure that came out of the tree slipped right through the net—like a thin mist!

I fell backward as dust swirled around us, and a terrifying voice cut through the chaos.

The dark shadow of an enormous chipmunk fell over us.

"HOW DARE YOU?!" the booming voice demanded. "Now you will feel the power of the Chipmunk!!"

CHAPTER 10

Interview with a Chipmunk

Dust swirled into a giant tornado. Everything became dark and scary.

But when the dust settled, I came face-to-face with . . . a tiny, nut-brown chipmunk.

I was so surprised, I almost fell off Izzy's head. *THIS* was the Monster of Acorn Island?!

She had a piece
of paper like mine
and was also using
it like a megaphone.

"YOU FOOLS!"
the chipmunk cried
out.

I bared my teeth. I could do it—I could
scare this tiny chipmunk! It would be so
easy!

But then I remembered how badly I felt
when I was scared.

I also wondered how the chipmunk had
made herself look like a giant chipmunk
before. Why did she feel like she needed to
be so scary?

I turned to Sweet Pea, my calm and caring
friend.

"I think you should do the talking," I said.

Sweet Pea smiled and croaked happily.

"Hi, I'm Sweet Pea the frog, and these are my friends. We want to know why you're hurting the forest," Sweet Pea explained.

"*I* AM NOT HURTING THE FOREST!" the chipmunk boomed. Then she did something surprising. She put down her paper megaphone. Now she just sounded like a regular chipmunk.

"I used to be a happy, daytime chipmunk. I loved the woods and everyone in them! But then humans came and left their trash EVERYWHERE. My family and I had to leave our nest—there was too much trash!" she said.

My jaw dropped to the ground. All this time I'd thought we were facing a giant evil monster. But this chipmunk wasn't evil at all. She actually cared a lot about the island.

"That must have been awful," Sweet Pea said.

"It was! After that, I was too scared to go out in the daytime. Small chipmunks like me were getting stuck in plastic wrapping and other trashed items. That's when I realized that humans were dangerous to us! So now I've promised to have my revenge. I'm going to drive everyone away so they can't hurt my home again," the chipmunk finished.

"There has to be another way," Sweet Pea said. "You can't do this alone."

"Oh, I'm not alone," the chipmunk said.

That's when I saw the shadows move. Suddenly, we were surrounded by chipmunks on all sides.

"I know you've been hurt, but our humans are different," Izzy said.

"You have to believe us!" I said.

"I'm sorry, but I can't. Humans need to be driven out of this forest once and for all. Luckily, I've found a way to be so scary, that their vacations will be ruined for good!" the chipmunk exclaimed.

Then, she let out a whistle, and the chipmunks around us sprang into action. They ran to her and jumped on each other's shoulders until they formed one GIANT monster.

Sweet Pea looked over at me, frozen in place. "I'm sorry, Ember! You were right. This chipmunk IS scary," she said.

But that's when I remembered something else Sweet Pea had said.

The Monster of Acorn Island *wasn't* evil. She was scared. Just like . . . me!

The enormous chipmunk took one step forward.

"WAIT!" I yelled.

The giant chipmunk froze.

"I know what it's like to be scared, and to feel like your only option is to be scary back," I said. "But please come with us. We have something to show you before you scare the humans away!"

CHAPTER 11

The Cleaning

The chipmunks had made a GIANT chipmunk-filled creature. The Monster of Acorn Island had come to life, and the evil chipmunk leader was directing them!

"All right, we'll give you a chance," the evil chipmunk said, after a long, terrible pause.

"But only if we ALL come with you," the evil chipmunk said as the giant monster got smaller.

I nodded confidently.

"Ember, what is your plan?" Izzy whispered.

"We need to show these chipmunks our humans don't want to hurt them," I replied. "It's okay. Trust me."

Izzy and Sweet Pea nodded. Then I led the chipmunks down the path.

I knew this was a risk. I was leading the chipmunks to my humans. If they wanted, the chipmunks could scare them all away, right there and then.

But I knew Lucy and her friends, and how much they cared about nature and doing the right thing.

So I led the chipmunks to where the humans were in the clearing. As we approached, we heard voices from behind the trees.

I took a deep breath and peered into the clearing.

The clearing looked different! It wasn't covered in trash anymore. Instead, I could see big patches of grass and flowers.

Arjun and Lia's mom were sorting the litter into recycling and trash bags, and Mr. and Mrs. Chin were combing the area for any trash left behind.

Kevin was writing in a notebook, and Lia's dad was sitting next to him. "We wrote a letter to ask about placing permanent recycling bins on this island," Kevin explained. "We want to send it to the mayor."

Lia and Lucy were making signs that said CLEAN UP and PLEASE RESPECT THE WOODS.

"Great job, everyone," Arjun's dad said as he carried a trash bag to the minivan.

"Yes, we're so proud of you and your teamwork," Mrs. Chin said.

The kids cheered. I felt my chest puff with pride. But was this enough to make the chipmunk decide not to scare our humans?

Sweet Pea, Izzy, and I turned to the evil chipmunk. Her eyes were wide.

"Oh wow, my oak tree! It looks nice and clean again. We can move back in!!" the chipmunk exclaimed, her eyes big and watery.

"Yes!" Sweet Pea said.

I grinned, and Izzy did a happy dance while the chipmunks celebrated.

"I'm sorry. I was wrong to scare everyone away. But I didn't know what else to do!" the chipmunk said, after a few minutes. "I'm Sesame, by the way."

"It's okay, Sesame," I said.

"We all make mistakes and feel scared sometimes," Sweet Pea said.

"And it's great to meet you!" Izzy said.

Sesame looked at us with a big smile. It turns out Sesame was, in fact, a very nice chipmunk. She was DEFINITELY a loyal sidekick I wanted on my team when I ruled the world.

We all spent the rest of the afternoon helping the humans. I helped Lucy finish her signs, and Sweet Pea sang Lia a song. Izzy danced around Arjun to encourage him as he cleaned up.

At the end of the day, the humans loaded the last of the trash and recycling into the van. My pet friends and I watched happily as Sesame and her family moved back into their tree.

"Great job, Ember," Sweet Pea said.

"No, it was YOUR plan to talk to the chipmunk instead of scare her. I'm sorry I didn't listen. *You* were right all along," I said.

"Well, we were a good team—" Sweet Pea began to say.

Then behind us we heard, "GASP!"

CHAPTER 12

Tasty, Tasty, Beautiful S'mores

Sweet Pea, Izzy, and I whirled around.

Behind us, Lucy was standing, holding a pile of long, thin branches.

"I found sticks for s'mores!" she said.

"Yay!" we cheered.

"Come on, everyone, time for a party," Lucy called to us.

We followed her back to the cabin.

That night, the humans had a big party to celebrate the end of the trip and all their cleanup efforts.

Mrs. Chin taught Lucy how to build a campfire.

Mr. Baptiste pet me and Izzy while Mr. Chin made the burgers.

Kevin proudly showed off the hamburger rolls he had baked with Mr. Ramanathan's help. Everyone else sang campfire songs with Mrs. Baptiste.

Later, when the humans were toasting s'mores around the campfire, Sesame, Greta, and Ollie joined us at the edge of the forest.

"I'm sorry I pretended to be evil and scared everyone," Sesame said to Greta and Ollie.

"That's okay, Sesame. We're sorry we didn't know about all the trash that was hurting you and your tree!" Ollie said.

"Yeah, if someone took my pond away, I'd be so upset and scared!" Greta said.

"I promise I won't scare humans anymore. But I WILL keep an eye out for people who litter and make sure to point out the new CLEAN UP sign," Sesame said.

"That sounds like a perfect plan," Greta said.

"I'll help you!" Ollie said.

"I guess it's time to give this up," Sesame said. She began to take off her evil cloak, which was made from an old dish towel.

"Wait," Sweet Pea said. "I have an idea. I got it from a book!"

"Sweet Pea gets amazing ideas from books!" I told the chipmunk. "You should ask her for reading recommendations."

Sweet Pea's happy croak filled the clearing.

"I know just what to do," she said.

It didn't take long at all.

And a few minutes later, Sesame proudly showed off her new costume. It wasn't an evil cloak anymore. It was a superhero cape!

"Now, you're the protector of the forest!"
Sweet Pea said. We all applauded, and then
celebrated by eating graham cracker crumbs.

"I can't wait to tell Steve and Neo all about
our adventures and new friends when we get
home," I said.

"And to hear about their adventures with
the pet sitter, too!" Izzy said.

"That reminds me," Ollie said. "The bird network has been trying to get in touch with you all."

"Oh, by the way, what is this bird network?" I asked. I remembered that Ollie had mentioned it before.

"It's how birds communicate! We carry messages from all over the world," Ollie explained. "Your bird friend, Neo, has been trying to send you a message. I don't know what it is, but a bird will soon find you . . ."

CHAPTER 13

Beware the Trash Can!

$\mathbb{T}$he next day, after breakfast, we packed up the cars.

Sesame, Ollie, Greta, and the rest of the chipmunks came to wave goodbye as we drove off.

My tail wagged as the trees sped by. I was so proud of us for finding out the true identity of the Monster of Acorn Island. And now I had so many new friends, and new allies, for when I rule the world.

We were on the bridge, this time leading away from Acorn Island, when the raven found us again.

"Ember!" the raven called. "I have a message from Neo! Ollie told me where to find you. There's trouble at home!"

"Oh no!" Izzy said.

"What is it?" I asked.

"Trash cans are mysteriously moving all over, and no pet is safe," the raven said.

My fur stood on end.

"The raccoons," the raven went on. "They're taking over the neighborhood!"

Susan Tan lives in Cambridge, Massachusetts. She grew up with lots of small dogs who all could rule the world. Susan is the author of the Cilla Lee-Jenkins series, and *Ghosts, Toast, and Other Hazards.* She enjoys knitting, crocheting, and petting every dog who will let her. Pets Rule! is her first early chapter book series.

Wendy Tan Shiau Wei is a Chinese-Malaysian illustrator based in Kuala Lumpur, Malaysia. Over the last few years, she has contributed to numerous animation productions and advertisements. Now her passion for storytelling has led her down a new path: illustrating children's books. When she's not drawing, Wendy likes to spend time playing with her mix-breed rescue dog, Lucky. The love for her dog is her inspiration to help this book come to life!

Questions & Activities

Before going on vacation to Acorn Island, the pugs warn Ember about an evil chipmunk. Why is this chipmunk known as the Monster of Acorn Island?

When a raven warns Ember, Sweet Pea, and Izzy about the Monster of Acorn Island again, they get worried. What plan do they come up with? Reread chapter 3.

Ember and his pet friends meet a frog named Greta. What does Greta tell them about the evil chipmunk? Reread page 42.

Ember and his pet friends meet Ollie, the wise owl. Ollie knows the evil chipmunk's secret weakness. What is it?

In chapter 12, Sesame's evil cloak turns into a superhero cape. Write and draw Sesame's superhero adventure story!